Book 2: VISION of FLAMES

CLAIRVOYANT CLAIRE

Spellbound

An Imprint of Magic Wagon
abdobooks.com

by JENNY SCOTT   ILLUSTRATED BY BILLY YONG

FOR GAVIN AND BELLA -JS

TO RACHEL, FOR ALWAYS BELIEVING IN ME -BY

abdobooks.com

Published by Magic Wagon, a division of ABDO, PO Box 398166,
Minneapolis, Minnesota 55439. Copyright © 2020 by Abdo Consulting Group,
Inc. International copyrights reserved in all countries. No part of this book
may be reproduced in any form without written permission from the publisher.
Spellbound™ is a trademark and logo of Magic Wagon.

Printed in the United States of America, North Mankato, Minnesota.

102019
012020

Written by Jenny Scott
Illustrated by Billy Yong
Edited by Tamara L. Britton
Art Directed by Christina Doffing

Library of Congress Control Number: 2019942289

Publisher's Cataloging-in-Publication Data

Names: Scott, Jenny, author. | Yong, Billy, illustrator.
Title: Vision of flames / by Jenny Scott ; illustrated by Billy Yong.
Description: Minneapolis, Minnesota : Magic Wagon, 2020. | Series: Clairvoyant Claire; book 2
Summary: Twelve-year-old Olivia is psychic! In a vision, she sees a local animal shelter catch fire. She
    and her friend Sebastian post the prediction on their blog Clairvoyant Claire. Though Olivia
    predicted the pirate treasure theft, people are still not convinced Clairvoyant Claire is legit. But
    public perception starts to change after a dramatic rescue.
Identifiers: ISBN 9781532136573 (lib. bdg.) | ISBN 9781532137174 (ebook) | ISBN 9781532137471
    (Read-to-Me ebook)
Subjects: LCSH: Clairvoyants--Juvenile fiction. | Blogs--Juvenile fiction. | Animal shelters--
    Juvenile fiction. | Buildings--Fires and fire prevention--Juvenile fiction. | Mystery and detective
    stories--Juvenile fiction. | Friendship--Juvenile fiction. | Self-confidence--Juvenile fiction.
Classification: DDC [Fic]--dc23

Table of Contents

CHAPTER 1

Furry Friends 4

CHAPTER 2

No More Time 16

CHAPTER 3

Dog Rescue 26

CHAPTER 4

Making New Friends 34

CHAPTER 1
Furry Friends

Sebastian and I are making sandwiches when I feel a VISION starting. Goose bumps PRICKLE up my arms. In a snap, I'm no longer slapping ham on a sandwich. Instead, I'm staring up at FurHaven Dog Shelter. And it's on FIRE!

When the VISION clears, I turn to Sebastian. "We need to **POST** a **PREDICTION** on Clairvoyant Claire's blog!"

CLAIRVOYANT CLAIRE

Dear Citizens of Edgewood,

I have a **NEW** prediction and it's a bad one. The FurHaven Dog Shelter is going to catch **FIRE** today at 12:23 p.m. while the director is out to lunch. Innocent dogs are in **DANGER**! We must act now!

Sincerely,

Clairvoyant Claire

FURHAVEN
DOG SHELTER

OPEN HOUSE

ven Open House

  WS   👍 30   👎 2   ↗ SHARE   ⇗ SAVE

Next...

Happy Dreams
- Sailor Rift

.OOK

"Your VISIONS are getting more serious, Olivia," Sebastian says after he hits PUBLISH.

"I know. I've never had a vision where someone could get HURT."

Sebastian shares Claire's prediction and we **WATCH** for comments. Clairvoyant Claire has gained some popularity after her first prediction came **TRUE**.

An hour *later*, there are twenty-three comments and Morgan Cooper, editor of *Edgey Press*, shares the POST.

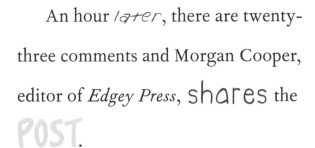 "Perhaps it's time we start believing," he says.

That's when Officer Ezra **chimes** in.

"Please know that we are taking this very seriously. We will continue to monitor the situation closely."

"Maybe the post has stopped the VISION from coming **TRUE**," Sebastian says.

CHAPTER 2
No More Time

I can't sit **still**. I haven't had

another VISION, but there is this

ICKY feeling in my stomach.

Sebastian **sits** at the

computer desk and refreshes Claire's

post. "Someone just saw the FurHaven

director ordering lunch at Jimmy's!"

Nothing happens.

"Maybe that's a GOOD thing?" Sebastian says.

But at 12:04 p.m., I get GOOSE BUMPS again. When I LOOK down, I'm standing behind FurHaven Dog Shelter at the fence with some kind of tool in my hands. I can smell the SMOKE from the fire. When I snap back, I turn to Sebastian. "What kind of tool would CUT through a fence?"

"Wire cutters."

"Help me **FIND** some."

In the garage, Sebastian RUMMAGES through a tool cabinet. "I found some! Now what?"

"Now we pedal hard. We're **RUNNING** out of time."

On the north side of town, we turn onto the LONG road that leads to the shelter. We hurry around back where two doggie doors LEAD from the building to a fenced-in yard. Several dogs are there waiting like they're PSYCHIC too.

"Hi, boy." I let one of the **BIG** dogs sniff my hand. "We're here to help."

Inside, a dog HOWLS loudly. Sebastian and I look up. SMOKE curls from a window. "Hurry!" I say. Sebastian and I start CUTTING.

CHAPTER 3
Dog Rescue

With each CLIP of the cutters, the hole gets **BIGGER**. A miniature goldendoodle manages to SLIP through. Two more dogs break free. Then another dog *wiggles* his way out, but the fence catches him on the side and he YELPS. The smoke thickens.

We finally **CUT** a hole through the fence that is half the size of us. **GRITTING** my teeth, I try to pull it back so the dogs don't **CUT** themselves as they escape.

A window breaks in the back of the shelter and **FLAMES** burst through.

What good is a psychic gift if someone or something gets hurt?

Sebastian and I hear a vehicle pull in at the same time and we start **Yelling**. "Back here! Help us!"

Four people come **RUNNING** around the building carrying giant wire **CUTTERS**. The FurHaven director runs after them. "Here," a man says and hands me a pair of **THICK** work gloves. "So you don't **CUT** your hands."

I **slip** them on and he clips at the fence with his *CUTTERS* like the fence is made of sticks, not metal. Two dogs **RUN** free, then four, then ten! The director starts rounding them up, **calling** them all by name. "I'm so sorry," he says. "I didn't believe in Clairvoyant Claire, but now I do."

We work together until all of the dogs are *LOOSE*.

CHAPTER 4
Making New Friends

The **FIRE** department arrives just seconds before the police. The firemen *clamor* out of the truck and unwind their hose and blast on the water. The flames sizzle and turn to smoke.

Two **BRAVE** firemen go inside the building to check for any dogs that might be stuck in kennels. When they come out, they're carrying a Dalmatian and a poodle.

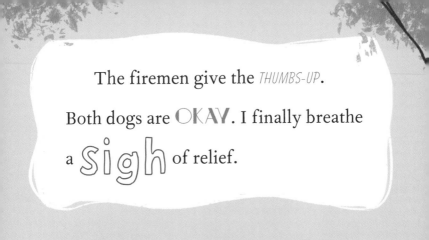

The firemen give the *THUMBS-UP*.

Both dogs are OKAY. I finally breathe

a Sigh of relief.

The little GOLDENDOODLE barks at my feet, so I duck down and scoop him up. He **LICKS** at my hand like he's thanking me.

"Hey," Sebastian *whispers*. "Police. Incoming!"

I look up as Officer Ezra walks over. "I heard you two were the FIRST on the scene."

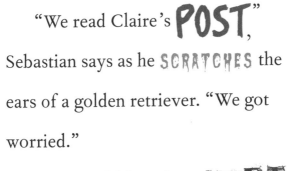

"We read Claire's **POST**," Sebastian says as he **SCRATCHES** the ears of a golden retriever. "We got worried."

"You could have been **HURT**."

"But we weren't," I say. "We couldn't just *leave* the dogs."

"Do you **KIDDOS** happen to know who Clairvoyant Claire is? Perhaps she's a friend or an adult you know? I would like to give her a proper thank-you."

Sebastian frowns real hard. "No. I don't think we know her."

The goldendoodle NUZZLES into my arms. "I wish I did know Claire. She seems really cool."

Officer Ezra *purses* her lips, her hands on her duty belt. She gives us a **LOOK** like maybe she knows we're not telling the whole TRUTH.

"Well, if you happen to learn her identity, *please* let me know."

That night, my new goldendoodle friend **lying** beside me, I get that shivery feeling that comes with a VISION.

My bedroom disappears and suddenly I'm in the police station. Officer Ezra **STANDS** in front of me. "I need Clairvoyant Claire's **HELP**," she says.